Dead Man's Close

by

Catherine MacPhail

Illustrated by Karen Donnelly

To all my boys,
with love

First published in 2006 in Great Britain by
Barrington Stoke Ltd
www.barringtonstoke.co.uk

ISBN-10: 1-84299-391-7
ISBN-13: 978-1-84299-391-0

Printed in Great Britain by Bell & Bain Ltd

Contents

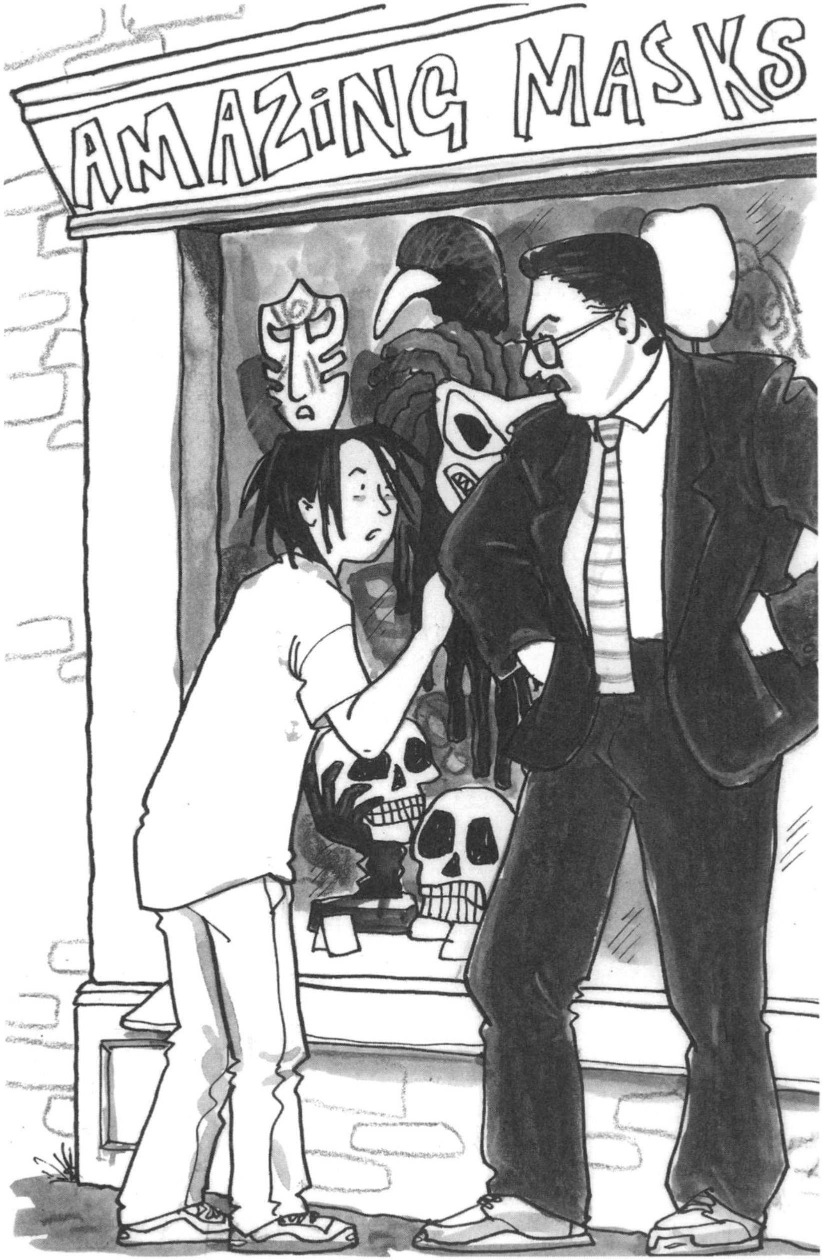
AMAZING MASKS

Chapter 1
Body Snatcher!

"Keep up with the rest of the class, Spider!" Mr Fisher's voice boomed out.

Spider was hanging back behind the others, looking in at one of the shops in Edinburgh's Old Town. He really liked the skeleton heads and the monster masks in the window.

"You and your monsters, Spider. Is that all you ever think about? This tour is about books. So many wonderful writers lived in Edinburgh, and still do."

Books, Spider thought glumly. *Boring!* He liked monsters better.

Mr Fisher pulled him on. "I lost you on the last school trip. I do not intend to lose you again."

He dragged Spider back to where the rest of the class were standing with Robby. Robby was their tour guide. "If it's monsters and weird stories you want, Spider," Robby said, "Old Edinburgh is full of them. Edinburgh has a very creepy history."

"Edinburgh?" Spider hadn't heard of any vampires or zombies roaming around Scotland, unless you counted his big brother and his pals.

"Have you heard of Burke and Hare?"

Spider thought about it. "Is that the two new teachers at our school?" he asked.

Mr Fisher tutted. "No. It is not!"

Robby went on. "Burke and Hare were body snatchers. The most famous body snatchers in history. In the 1800s there were lots of medical schools in Edinburgh. Doctors went there to be trained. All the schools needed dead bodies for medical experiments."

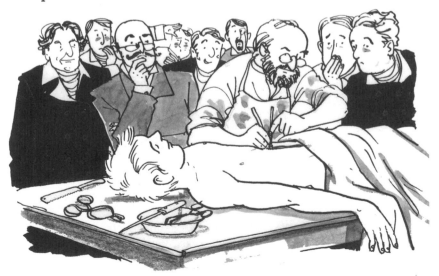

"Medical ... what?"

Mr Fisher said, "The medical students needed bodies so they could cut them up and study them, Spider."

"Cut them up?" Spider grinned. "So, instead of resting in peace, they would be resting in pieces!"

Everyone laughed when Spider said that. Everyone except Mr Fisher.

Mr Fisher never thought Spider's jokes were funny.

"Anyway," Robby went on. "The law said that only the bodies of criminals who had been hanged could be used for experiments. There were never enough bodies. So criminals began to dig fresh bodies up from graves and sell them to the medical schools. It was a good way to make money."

Spider began to get interested. Dead bodies, dug up from the grave. Sounded like a good old zombie story to him.

"Grave robbing became big business," Robby said. "So many graves were robbed that people paid to protect the graveyards. They put up watch towers and paid for guards. You can still see those towers today.

Then, along came Burke and Hare. They thought up an even easier way to make money. Digging up bodies was too much like hard work. So they roamed the streets of Edinburgh looking for *live* bodies. They picked on the poor, the homeless, people no one would miss. They killed them and took their bodies to a famous doctor, Doctor Knox. Doctor Knox gave them good money for the bodies."

Robby spoke in a creepy whisper. "Can you picture it? Not the Edinburgh of today, with its buses and traffic. But an Edinburgh of cobbled streets and narrow alleys. We call those alleys 'Closes' in the Old Town. It's a dark and foggy night. Burke and Hare push a cart over the cobbles. Suddenly, the cart hits a bump and an arm dangles out from beneath a cover. Burke and Hare look all around to make sure no one else has seen, and then they shove the arm back under the cover and move on."

The rest of the class had come up round Robbie to listen. "Did the police get them in the end?" Spider asked.

"Yes, Burke and Hare were both arrested. But Hare didn't go to the gallows. He wasn't hanged. He saved himself by giving the police all the proof they needed to hang his partner in crime, Burke."

"You mean, Hare grassed on his mate?" Spider asked.

"Yes, indeed. And do you know what happened to Burke's body?"

Spider shook his head.

"After he was hanged, *his* body was sent to the medical school."

"So he was cut up and used by the doctors too?'

"He was," Robby said. "In fact, they made his skin into a notebook. You can see it in the Police Museum. And his skeleton still hangs in the University."

"Can we go and see them, sir?" Spider asked.

Mr Fisher shook his head. "You're a very odd boy, Spider."

Spider grinned. "Thank you, sir."

The class moved on. Spider had liked the story of Burke and Hare. The Old Town of Edinburgh was creepy. They were in Fleshmarket Close now. Even the names of the narrow streets made him shiver.

He saw his sister, Lizzie, walking alone, at the back of the class. Spider smiled. He was going to play a trick on her. He slipped into a dark doorway and waited.

As Lizzie strolled past, Spider grabbed her. "Gotcha!"

But Lizzie punched him so hard he fell back. With a yell Spider tumbled down a long flight of stairs.

He blacked out. He saw a band of stars and in the middle of them was Lizzie, yelling. "Spider! Are you OK? Talk to me."

Spider sat up and rubbed his head. "Are you trying to kill me, Lizzie?"

"What you did was stupid! Robby's just been telling us about body snatchers and then you jump out of the dark and try to snatch me! Of course I'm going to punch you back!" She pulled him to his feet. "Come on. We better catch up."

They headed back to the street.

But there was no street. Just another dark alley. "We must have taken a wrong turn," Lizzie moaned.

Spider didn't think so. A thick fog had come down on the Old Town. There was no sound of traffic. All he could hear was a dog barking somewhere nearby.

"Lizzie," Spider said. "I've got a really bad feeling about this."

Chapter 2
The Time Lord

Spider had a funny feeling. On the last school outing, when Lizzie and Spider's class went round Edinburgh Castle, they'd gone back in time to Old Edinburgh. Were they back in time again?

"How did it happen, Spider? Are we in Old Edinburgh again? You didn't even say '*I wish*' five times, like the last time."

Suddenly Spider knew exactly how it had happened. He didn't need to *say* anything to be transported back to the past.

"I think I'm a Time Lord," he said. "Like Doctor Who."

Lizzie was not impressed. "I think you're a dipstick." She grabbed him by the neck. For a little sister, Lizzie was pretty strong. "Now get us back. I don't like it here."

Spider didn't like it either. He remembered Robby's story of Burke and Hare and he shivered. He made up his mind that no one was going to snatch his body.

"I'll look after you, Lizzie."

"You're the one who needs looking after! Every time I go out with you, we always end up getting lost."

At that instant, they heard a scream through the fog, as if someone was being murdered.

Then a gruff voice roared, "I bet your father would pay a lot of money to get you back, boy!"

They heard a boy begging. "Let me go," he croaked.

Spider and Lizzie peeked round the corner. In another dark alley there was a big brute of a man. He had a grip on a boy, just about Spider's age. The big man was lifting him off the ground, ready to hit him with the stick he had in his hand.

The boy was coughing and trying to shake himself free.

"Come on, Lizzie," Spider shouted. They ran. Spider jumped on the man's back.

Lizzie sunk her teeth into his hand.

The man yelled and lost his grip, and the boy fell to the ground in a heap.

The man spun round, ready to fight. He had a mouthful of black and broken teeth. Spider kicked him hard on the shins and the man tripped and fell. He landed with a splat in a pile of dog mess. Spider wanted to laugh, but he didn't have time.

The boy pulled them on. "Let's get out of here!" Spider didn't need to be told twice.

They all ran together, through the narrow closes. They could hear the man behind them yelling. He was calling his mates to help him.

The boy was gasping for breath. It was Lizzie who made him stop running. "Are you OK?" she asked.

"Am I what?" He smiled at them. "Thank you for helping me. My name is Lewis."

He held out his hand to Spider.

"And I'm Spider, and that's my sister Lizzie."

Lewis coughed again. "I'll be fine in a minute."

"Haven't you got an inhaler?" Lizzie asked him.

Lewis didn't understand. "What's an inhaler?"

Spider saw then how thin and pale the boy was. His face was almost white. Spider helped him to sit down.

"I should not run," Lewis said. "My chest is always bad."

"Who was that man?"

Lewis shook his head. "I don't know. But the Old Town is full of bad men. Villains. That one saw my fine coat and thought he could hold me for ransom. My father would have to pay to get me back."

"You mean he was going to kidnap you!"

They heard the faint shouts through the fog. The man had got a gang together, and they were all coming after them.

"Yes, and he still might, if he catches us," Lewis gasped.

"If it's so dangerous, what are you doing here?" Spider asked.

Lewis said softly, "I am following a man with a secret life. He may even be a murderer."

Chapter 3
The Secret Life

A man with a secret life, a murderer maybe – this was Spider's kind of story. "A secret life? Who do you think he's murdered?" Spider wanted to know more.

"I don't know. But he comes here every night. Perhaps he's murdered lots of people."

"You mean, he's a serial killer ... like Jack the Ripper?"

Lewis looked as if he didn't know what Spider was talking about. "What's a serial killer? Who's Jack the Ripper?"

Spider was just about to tell him but Lizzie shut him up. "What year is this, Lewis?" Lizzie asked.

"You don't know what year this is?" That made Lewis laugh. "It's 1861, of course."

Lizzie flopped down on some stairs at the end of the street. "You've done it again, Spider," she said.

"Spider – that's a wonderful name," said Lewis as he sat down next to her. "I wish I had an interesting name."

Spider was proud of his nickname too. His friends gave him that nickname because, like Robert the Bruce's spider, he never gave up. When he wanted to do something, he tried and tried until in the end he'd done it. "Oh well, Lewis," Spider said, "maybe you'll do something and make your name famous someday."

Lewis stood up. "That's why I'm following this man. I want to find out the truth about him. Get the police to arrest him. Then my name'll be in the papers and I'll be famous."

"Do you want to be a great detective … like Sherlock Holmes?" Spider asked.

"Who's Sherlock Holmes?"

Lizzie whispered to her brother, "He hasn't been written about yet, stupid. Lewis won't have heard of him."

Spider tried to cover up his mistake. "Oh – Sherlock Holmes is just one of my uncles," he said.

Lewis was impressed. "What a great name – Sherlock Holmes," he said.

"Great names run in the family," Spider said.

Lizzie knew then that Lewis and her brother were two of a kind. One was as daft as the other.

"Tell us about this man. The one you're following," Spider said softly.

"He lives on my street. And I know he has a secret life. By day, he's a doctor, everyone in the town respects him. But by night, every night, he leaves his house and comes to the Old Town. I want to know why. He has a secret and I mean to find out what it is."

"He sounds just like the man in the story about Doctor Jekyll and Mr Hyde," Spider said.

Once again Lewis looked puzzled. "Doctor who?"

Spider laughed. "No, not Doctor Who ..." Then he remembered that Lewis wouldn't know him either. "No, Lewis, Doctor Jekyll and Mr Hyde is a great story about this doctor who takes a drug and it turns him into a monster. The monster's name is Mr Hyde. By night, Mr Hyde roams the streets doing terrible things, and in the morning he's Doctor Jekyll again and can't remember what he's done. Just like your doctor. By day, one thing ... by night ... who knows?"

Lewis's eyes almost popped out of his head. "That's a wonderful story. I wish I'd written it. I'd love to be a writer, but my father won't hear of it. Thinks it's a stupid idea. He wants me to be an engineer like him, and his father too."

Lizzie was impressed. "I'd love to be an engineer," she said.

Lewis laughed. "Lizzie, you're a girl. You could not be an engineer." Then he looked at what Lizzie was wearing. Trousers. "You *are* a girl, aren't you?"

Now it was Lizzie's turn to laugh. "Of course I'm a girl. And where I come from, Lewis, girls can be anything they want to be." Lizzie was suddenly very glad to be living in the 21st century – if she ever got back there, that was.

Just then a door opened in one of the tall old narrow houses. A ribbon of light lit the cobbles in the street. The doctor came out. He had his bag with him and he shut the door softly behind him.

He looked all about, as if he was checking that no one was watching him.

Then he pulled his cloak around him, and moved off down the street.

"He does look dodgy," Spider muttered.

"He has something to hide," Lewis said. "Let's go after him."

Spider didn't need to be asked.

Lizzie gave a sigh. "I'd better come as well. I think you two'll need my help."

Chapter 4
An Empty Coffin

They darted in and out of the dark alleys as they tried to follow the strange doctor. All the time, in the fog, they could hear the shouts of the gang of men who were still coming after them. Spider was loving it. He had forgotten everything else. It was Lizzie who was scared that they were getting more and more lost.

"We're miles away from where we started. We'll never get back," she said.

"No, we're still in the Old Town. I'll get you back to where you came from," Lewis told her.

"I don't like it here," Lizzie said.

Lewis was shocked. "I love the Old Town, the old buildings, the narrow streets."

"It's smelly," Lizzie said.

"Not as smelly as it used to be," Lewis told her. "You had to be very careful in these closes and alleys in the old days. The people who lived on the top floors used to throw every kind of rubbish out of the windows."

"What do you mean?" Lizzie asked. "Every kind of rubbish?"

"Well," Lewis said, "there were no inside toilets, so everything went out the window. And I mean everything." Lewis pretended to be sick on the street.

Spider giggled. "I wouldn't like to be walking in the street when that came down. You'd have poo all over you."

Lewis laughed too. "It got so bad that they made a rule you could only throw things out of your window when the town clock struck ten at night. So as soon as the clock struck ten, the windows opened and down it all came."

He grinned at Spider. "It must have been great fun to watch everybody jumping about to miss all the stuff being thrown down onto the streets."

"Trust boys to think that would be funny!" Lizzie said.

"They had to shout, 'Gardez loo!' to warn people below," Lewis said. "That's French for 'watch out below'."

"You must be really clever to know French," Lizzie said.

"My father says I know too much of the wrong things ... but these are interesting facts. I love reading. Do you love books too, Spider?"

"As long as there's a monster in them," Spider said.

Lewis grinned. "I'd love to write a monster story."

"Or a pirate story, I love pirates," Spider went on.

Lewis looked at him. "We have so much in common, Spider."

Just then they saw the doctor again. He was coming out of another house on the corner of the close they were in. "One thing by day," Lewis said softly, "and another by night."

"He has a secret life," Spider said.

Lizzie tutted. "A secret life! Rubbish!"

"It has happened before, Lizzie," said Lewis. "There was a man who lived in Edinburgh a hundred years ago. His name was Deacon Brodie. He was a carpenter and very good at it. We have one of his cabinets

in our house. He worked for many of the rich people of the town. No one knew that by night he and his gang of thieves would break into their houses and rob them."

"Like Robin Hood?" Spider asked. "Did he give the money to the poor?"

Lewis shook his head. "No, not like Robin Hood. Deacon Brodie kept all the money for himself. But no one knew about his secret life. Until the police caught him one night."

"A double life too, just like Jekyll and Hyde," Spider said, almost to himself.

"In the end, Deacon Brodie was hanged. And the gallows he was hanged on were ones that he'd designed himself – before people knew about his double life," Lewis went on.

"So that was the end of Deacon Brodie," Spider said.

"Or was it, Spider?" Lewis spoke very softly. "The story goes that he did survive, that he was seen years later in Paris. And when his coffin was opened ... his body was missing!"

They watched the doctor as he moved on to the next house. Lewis peered at him. "Is he turning into a monster yet?" he asked.

Spider stared too. "No, not yet. But it's bound to happen soon."

Lizzie gave a sigh. Both those boys were mad. "This is crazy," she said. She looked at Lewis and Spider. They were crazy too.

Chapter 5
Mary King's Close

"What we're doing is very dangerous," Lizzie said. "It's a stupid idea to follow a man you don't know anything about. And at night, too!"

"But I do know something about this man," Lewis said. "He lives on my street. And he's a doctor."

"You said he was a killer," Lizzie hissed. "That seems pretty dangerous to me."

The doctor was knocking at the door of yet another house. A moment later the door opened. Without a word the doctor stepped inside.

"Why is he visiting all these houses?" Lewis said.

"Maybe he's blackmailing the people in them. Are they giving him money to keep their secrets?" Spider said.

"People here don't have any money. This is the poorest part of town. In fact, we are close to a very creepy part of the Old Town. Mary King's Close. Do you know the story of Mary King's Close?"

"No," Spider said. "Never heard of it."

One thing about Lewis, Lizzie thought, *he knows how to tell a good story.*

"In 1645," Lewis began, "some people in Mary King's Close fell sick with the plague. Everyone was so afraid that the plague would spread that they shut in the people who lived there, the sick *and* the well, the living *and* the dead. They walled them up and left them all to die. The story goes that their screams and cries for help could be heard for days and nights. It was terrible. Then, at last, the screams stopped."

"Do you mean those people were just left there to die? That's awful," Spider said.

Lewis went on. "For years, no one lived in Mary King's Close, until at last one brave family moved in. The first night they awoke and saw bits of bodies, hands and feet and heads that were floating around the room. The spirits of the dead of Mary King's Close."

Lewis spoke in a soft voice. "The man of the family plucked up his courage and held out his hand to the spirit hand that was floating in front of him."

Lizzie tutted. "What happened then? Did the spirits vanish when he shook the ghost hand?"

Lewis nodded. "Never to be seen again."

"Wow!" Spider said. "I would never be brave enough to shake a ghost hand."

"Nor me, Spider," Lewis said.

Lizzie already knew the story of Mary King's Close. She'd asked Robby about it and he'd said it was just a tall tale. But what was the point of saying anything?

They were so lost in the story they hadn't heard the sounds of feet thudding towards them. Now, it was almost too late to get away.

The big man with the broken teeth was the first to spot the children. "There they are!"

Spider grabbed Lizzie and Lewis. "Run!"

Chapter 6
Chase!

"Can you keep up, Lizzie?" Lewis called.

"Keep up?' she shouted. "I'm faster than you!" She sprinted past them both. Now it was the boys who had to keep up with her.

"I should have told you, she's a really fast runner," Spider said.

Lewis began to fall behind. He couldn't stop coughing. "Go on without me," he muttered. "Save yourselves."

Lizzie had had enough. "Save yourselves? What are you on about?" She ran back and grabbed Lewis's arm. "Help me, Spider." Spider grabbed his other arm and they lifted Lewis up and ran on.

But Lewis was holding them back. The gang running after them was catching up. Spider began to get really scared.

What if the gang did kidnap them and took them onto pirate ships? Spider had once said he'd love that to happen. Now he wasn't so sure.

Lewis was scared too. "I think I'd rather write adventures than live them," he puffed. He began to cough again. "I've got to stop. I've just got to."

Spider spotted a dark doorway. "Let's hide in here."

They huddled down and Lizzie covered them with papers and rubbish. Maybe the men wouldn't see them and would run on by.

"Don't even breathe," she whispered.

"Now I know how homeless people feel," Spider said. He was shivering with cold and fear.

They could hear the men's feet getting closer and hear their angry shouts. "Where did they go?" the men were yelling. "They've got to be here somewhere."

The gang stopped in front of the doorway where Spider, Lewis and Lizzie had hidden. Spider began to shake. He gripped Lizzie's hand. His mother was going to kill him if he got Lizzie kidnapped.

"Over here!" one of them shouted. "I saw someone run down this alley."

Spider almost cheered. They were moving off!

And that was when Lewis began to cough again. He had tried to hold his breath and that had only made things worse. Lewis coughed so hard Spider thought he was going to be sick.

"What was that?" a big man grunted.

Spider could see how hard Lewis was trying to hold his breath. But it was no good.

"Sorry," Lewis said softly, and he coughed again.

The men rushed back to the doorway. They ripped back the papers and rubbish. Broken Teeth grinned. He reminded Spider of a skull.

"Gotcha, my fine laddies!"

Chapter 7
Safe!

Broken Teeth turned to his gang. All the thugs grinned. "These three should fetch a few bob, eh, boys?"

Spider felt in his pockets for his mobile phone. It had got him out of a fix before. But it wasn't there. He hadn't got it this time!

They were done for.

"Leave those children be!" The booming voice came out of the fog.

A man, the doctor they had been following, was suddenly running toward them, and he was holding his stick up over his head. "Take your hands off them or I will have the law on you!" he shouted.

There was the sound of a whistle blowing through the fog, and the gang stepped back. Maybe they thought the police were there too. Then they were off, faster than you could say "body snatcher"!

Broken Teeth was suddenly left on his own. "I was only going to teach these boys a lesson!" he muttered.

"Be off with you!" the doctor said.

Broken Teeth didn't move, and for a moment, Spider was afraid he was going to start a fight with the doctor. But he didn't. He spat at their feet, and ran off into the fog.

"Are you all right?" The doctor looked at Lewis. "Wait a minute, I know you. You live in Heriot Row, don't you?"

Even in the dark, Spider could see Lewis
blush.

"Yes sir," he said.

"What are you doing here?" He looked at
Spider and Lizzie. "What are you all doing
here in the Old Town? At this time of
night?" He didn't wait for an answer.
"Doesn't matter now. Lucky for you I was

here. I come and tend to the poor people who live here and there's a bout of flu going round at the moment."

"Is that why you come here every night?" Lewis asked.

Lizzie tutted. "And you thought he was a murderer!" she whispered.

"Come on – I'm taking you home," the doctor said. "Your parents will be worried about you." The doctor helped Lewis to his feet. "I'll go and get us a cab. Just wait here."

"So much for my wonderful story," Lewis said, as the doctor left them to get the cab. "By day, he's a respectable doctor, by night ... he's an even better doctor."

"But it would still make a great story, Lewis – a double life. You should write it."

"I think I will, Spider ... what was the name of that story you told me about?"

"Doctor Jekyll and Mr Hyde. It's brilliant, Lewis," Spider said.

They walked to the end of the street. A horse-drawn cab was waiting. "Where shall I take you two?" the doctor asked Lizzie and Spider.

Spider looked up at the sign on the wall. Fleshmarket Close. They were back where they had started. "No, we'll walk from here. It's not far. We'll be OK," he said.

He just hoped that was true.

Lewis shook Spider's hand. "It was great meeting you both, and I have made up my mind, Spider. I want to have a great name too. Lewis is my middle name. I'm going to change the spelling, to something more interesting. How about L-o-u-i-s? Robert Louis Stevenson – that's a much better name for a writer, don't you think? It'll look good on the cover of a book."

Chapter 8
Lizzie Saves the Day!

Spider turned to his sister. "I've heard that name somewhere before, Lizzie," he said.

Lizzie had her mouth open in shock. "That's because Robert Louis Stevenson was the person who wrote Doctor Jekyll and Mr Hyde. And we've just met him ..."

"Wait a minute – are you saying that it was Lewis who wrote the Doctor Jekyll story?" Spider asked.

Lizzie was nodding her head. "We've just met a famous writer."

That wasn't what was bothering Spider. "But he went and wrote *my* story! I'm the one who gave him the idea for Doctor Jekyll and Mr Hyde ... hey, that's stealing!"

"You talk such a load of rubbish, Spider. You only know about that story because he wrote it in the first place."

"But it was me who gave him the idea," Spider said.

"Only because you'd read his book," Lizzie said.

Spider sat down and put his head in his hands. "Oh Lizzie, this going back in time is getting me totally mixed up."

"Let's go home, Spider," begged Lizzie.

If only I knew how, Spider thought. It should be easy, what with him being a Time Lord and everything. But no matter what he did they were still stuck in Fleshmarket Close, in the fog, in 1861.

"I'll get us back!' Lizzie said, giving him a punch on the arm. Spider never hit his little sister, so why was it all right for her to punch him?

"You can't, Lizzie. I'm the Time Lord."

Lizzie stood up tall and yelled at the top of her voice, "I insist we are taken back to our own time. Right! Now!"

They waited for the fog to lift. They listened for a crack of thunder. But nothing happened.

Spider gave a sigh. It wasn't going to work. Lizzie didn't have his special powers.

Suddenly, a familiar voice boomed out at them. "Where have you two been?"

It was Mr Fisher. Robby and the rest of the class came running up behind him. Spider had never been so glad to see anyone. "We're back! Lizzie, we're back!"

Lizzie grinned. "Who's the Time Lord now, smarty pants?"

Mr Fisher grabbed Spider by the collar. "You are in trouble again, Spider."

Big deal, Spider was thinking, he was always in trouble.

"We went back in time, sir," he said. "And do you know who we met? Robert Louis Stevenson."

"None of your lies, boy," Mr Fisher snapped.

Robby butted in. "No, it could be the truth. Lots of the tours round the Old Town have actors dressing up as famous people. Why, you might even meet Deacon Brodie, or Burke and Hare."

Spider looked at Lizzie. Was that the answer? Maybe they hadn't gone back to 1861 after all. Maybe they had only met some actors ...

He gave up on that idea fast. It was much more exciting to think they had gone back in time ... again.

"Just think, Lizzie," he whispered to his sister. "We met Robert Louis Stevenson."

Lizzie whispered back, "And he was every bit as daft as you."

Spider took no notice. "And I still say he stole my story."

Spider's Notebook

Doctors need dead bodies to examine and cut up. That way they can see how bodies work and how the bits of the body fit together.

About 200 years ago, there were not enough dead bodies for all the medical schools. That was because they only let doctors use the dead bodies of criminals who had been hanged.

Burke and Hare were two crooks who lived in Edinburgh and saw a good way of making some money — by getting hold of dead bodies and selling them to medical schools!

Other gangs dug up bodies from the graveyards and sold them. Burke and Hare had a better idea. They just killed people no one would miss and

took their bodies along to the medical schools to sell.

In the end Burke and Hare were caught.

And after that, there was a new law. Medical schools could use dead bodies if the families of people who had died said it was OK, or if people left their bodies in their wills.

That was the end of graveyard robbing and the body snatchers. So something good came of something bad.

Everything's different now. You can still leave your body for doctors and scientists to examine. Interested, sir?

No, thank you, Spider.

You can offer to give away any of your organs, sir, your kidneys, your eyes. You can give them to people who are still alive but whose organs don't work properly. We even have heart transplants. Healthy organs from people who have just died can save lives. My mum and dad carry donor cards, sir.

So do I, Spider.

The gift of life, my dad calls it. Funny how things change, sir.

It's all to do with progress and choice, Spider.

You know, sir, back in olden times, people had to pay to see a doctor. If you were too poor you would just die if someone didn't help you out. I asked my mum how it felt to live in the olden days, and she told me not to be so cheeky!

In 1946 the Labour Government started the NHS, the National Health Service. Everyone could have free health care. I think that's a great idea, sir.

There was a children's song about Burke and Hare.

Up the Close and Down the Stair

In the house with Burke and Hare

Burke's the Butcher

Hare's the Thief

Knox the man who buys the beef.

What a yukky song to sing while you're playing sir!

You would never do that, would you, Spider?

Me, sir? No way, sir.

Burke and Hare worked at night. So did Deacon Brodie. Deacon Brodie was a carpenter by day but a robber by night. Then there was Major Thomas Weir. He was someone else with a double life. By day, he was such a holy man people said he was one of the Bowhead Saints. But by night he was evil and his nickname was the Wizard of West Bow. He did terrible things at night.

People say his ghost still haunts the town. He rides a headless horse, his face set in a terrible silent scream. (I mean Major Weir's face, sir, not the horse. It's not got a head, remember?) If it was a headless horse, sir, how could it see where it was going? It would keep bumping into things, wouldn't it?

BOOKS AND MONSTERS

I met Robert Louis Stevenson when Lizzie and I went back in time. He was a little boy when we met him and everyone called him Lewis.

what did I tell you about making up stories, Spider?

He was born in 1850, and he really did live in Heriot Row, Edinburgh. His father and grandfather

planned and built lighthouses. They
wanted Lewis to carry on their work.
But Lewis always wanted to be a
writer. He loved adventures, just like

me. He wrote
Treasure Island
about a boy who was
kidnapped by pirates.

Then he wrote
Kidnapped about a
boy, well, who gets kidnapped. He
even wrote a short story called The
Body Snatchers. His most famous
book was The Strange Case of Dr
Jekyll and Mr Hyde and he got the
idea from the story of Deacon Brodie.
Lewis loved the idea of a double life.
One thing by day, another by night.

(But I still say he stole the story from me.)

Spider, can't you understand? *He wrote that story before you were born!* - Lizzie.

Lewis had tuberculosis and was always ill. Tuberculosis is a terrible illness that affects your lungs. You cough up blood and can't breathe. At the end of his life, Lewis went to live in the island of Samoa on the South Seas. The hot climate was better for him.

He always wanted to go back to Scotland, but he died before he could do that. He died on 3 December 1894. He loved Scottish history, sir, and so do I.

If they had had inhalers then, sir, his life would have been a lot better. You don't need to die of tuberculosis now, sir. If only they'd known as much then as we know now, Lewis would have lived a lot longer.

There were other famous writers who lived in Edinburgh at the same time as Lewis.

Sir Arthur Conan Doyle.

I am impressed, Spider.

He was a doctor too, sir. You can't get away from doctors, can you? He wrote lots of stories, but his most famous ones were about the great detective, Sherlock Holmes. And one of his most famous stories was The Hound of the Baskervilles. That was about a hound of hell. (That just means a big scary dog, sir.)

Thank you, Spider, I would never have known.

This hound roams the moors at night and chases people and then tears them apart with its teeth.

Lovely description, Spider.

See, writers love monsters. Maybe I should be a writer.

One of the most famous monster stories was written by a woman.

And *it's* the best!

That was Lizzie sir. Don't listen to her.

The book was called Frankenstein.

Frankenstein, by the way, was the name of the doctor, not the monster. Not a lot of people know that. The monster never really had a name in the book. Doctor Frankenstein wanted to make a human being so he put bits of different dead bodies together.

(We're back to body snatching, sir, and transplants. I'm very clever the way I link all this up, aren't I, sir?)

You're a genius, Spider.

The idea for Frankenstein came one day in 1816 when Mary Shelley and her husband and a doctor (doctors again, sir) had a contest to see who could write the scariest monster story. Mary Shelley won!

And she was the woman!

Shut up, Lizzie!

The doctor's story was about a vampire.

But the most famous vampire story was written by Bram Stoker who was Irish.

Bram Stoker wrote the story of Dracula.

Some people say the real Dracula was a prince called Vlad the Impaler. (I'll not tell you what he was famous for, sir. It would make you feel really, really sick.) But others think that Bram Stoker got the idea

for Dracula from Irish stories about
monsters who drank people's blood.

Everyone
knows about
Dracula now,
don't they, sir?

PLAGUES AND DEADLY DISEASES.

There's always been terrible plagues sir. Right from Bible times with the plagues of Egypt.

But one of the worst plagues was the Black Death in the 14th century. It killed one third of the people in Europe and Asia.

I'm learning something new every day, spider.

The plague was called the Black Death because if

you had it, your skin turned black. And they said it was black rats that passed it on. Yuk! The Black Death was one of the world's worst serial killers, sir.

Then there was also the Great Plague of London in 1665 to 1666. That killed thousands of people. If you had the Plague, they would paint a cross on the door of your house and everyone who lived there had to stay inside. At night, men would go round the streets with a cart and shout, "Bring Out Your Dead!"

And they would all chuck the dead bodies out the door.

can't you think of a better word than "chuck", Spider?

If you think that's bad, sir, you should hear about the battles in the Middle Ages! Armies chucked people who had the plague across into the middle of the enemy.

That's germ warfare! The very first case of it ever.

Do we need to know all that, Spider?

It's a really interesting fact, sir.

Since the start of time, there've been lots of epidemics. That's when hundreds of people get ill with the same disease.

There's been Cholera,

Smallpox,

Measles,

And flu as well! You wouldn't believe the number of people that have died of flu over the years. In 1918 Spanish flu killed 25 million people.

There aren't those deadly diseases now. We can get a jab or a medicine for them. But there are still other diseases that doctors are still working out how to cure, like AIDS and cancer. And now we're all scared of Bird Flu.

All this talk of diseases has depressed me, sir. On my next page I'm going back to something a bit more fun.

Monsters.

MYTHS AND MONSTERS

Do monsters really exist?

Stupid question, of course they do.

You only have to look in the mirror to see one.

Very funny, Lizzie.

We have our very own monster in Scotland. Nessie. The Loch Ness Monster.

Does she really exist?

Well, I know she does. My uncle Jimmy saw her.

Spider, he told us later it was our Auntie Morag in for a swim. - Lizzie

Easy mistake to make when you see the size of our Auntie Morag.

The first person to see Nessie and  write about it was Saint Columba. He wouldn't lie, would he, sir, because he was a saint!

Nessie has been seen lots of times since then. There's even been a famous photo. But people still think it's a hoax. They don't believe any of it.

There are stories about monsters all around the world.

It must be great to be in China. Because they have loads of monsters. Giant fish, called Kun that turn into giant birds when they fly.

And B-She, a snake that eats elephants.

I wouldn't like to meet that on a dark night. How big a snake must that be!

But my favourite monster is the Hopping Corpse.

why doesn't that surprise me, Spider?

That takes us right back to the beginning, sir, and the body snatching. The dead body is stolen from the grave and hops everywhere. (I don't know why it hops, by the way.) And it drinks blood. It's the nearest thing to a zombie I could find.

I knew you'd get a zombie in here somewhere.

Vampires turn up a lot in stories, too.

In India they have the story of the goddess Kali. She had fangs and wore a necklace made of corpses and skulls. She had four arms and she had a big fight with a great demon and drank all his blood and won. (The four arms must have been a big help.)

The Caribbean has some great stories about vampires. They have a story about a vampire that by day is an old woman but by night is a flying ball of fire.

Sounds like wee Mrs Jones who lives next door to us. - Lizzie

You know, sir, I think every country has different monster stories. Everyone could ask their mums and dads or their grannies. We come from all over the world and we've all got our own monster stories. My granny came from the Highlands and I'm going to ask her tonight. How about if we got all our stories together and

see who comes up with the best
monster?

*That's a very good idea,
Spider.*

But I've kept my best idea till
last, sir. You'll like this.

The Tales of the Arabian Nights.

There was a King in Arabia who
got married to a new wife every day
and then had the new wife killed the
next morning. (Not a very nice man,
eh?) Anyway, one day he married
Shahrazad. (Her name's got lots of
different spellings sir, but that's the
one I like best.)

Shahrazad told the King lots of stories. He liked stories. Every night she told him a different one, and she always ended at a very exciting bit, a cliffhanger.

(That's the way you always tell us to write a story, sir. End on a cliffhanger. I love cliffhangers! You want to know what happens next.)

The king didn't have Shahrazad killed because he always wanted to know the next part of her story. She was one clever lady!

She told some great stories, sir. Sinbad the Sailor, Ali Baba and the Forty Thieves, and Aladdin and the Magic Lamp.

Did you know, sir, that Robert Louis Stevenson wrote a book of short stories called *The New Arabian Nights*?

You know what I think? I think it's stories that keep the whole world together. From Lewis looking for monsters in Edinburgh, to Shahrazad telling stories about magic lamps in Arabia.

Everyone loves a good story.

I have hopes for you yet, Spider.

And everybody loves a good monster.

I think the world is ready for a good zombie story, sir. I'm going home to write mine tonight and I'll end it on a cliffhanger!

AUTHOR FACT FILE
CATHERINE MACPHAIL

Who is your favourite villain from a book or film?
Dracula, because I love vampires and there is no more evil vampire than Dracula.
Do you believe in ghosts/aliens/ monsters – any of the above?
I'm sure I've seen a UFO, it was certainly an unidentified flying object, but whether it came from another planet I don't know.
What's the spookiest thing that has happened to you?
One night my husband and I were driving along a lonely country road. Suddenly, an old tramp jumped out in front of us, we had to swerve to avoid him. I made my husband reverse, sure we must have hit him, and there was no sign of anyone there. Later, we heard that the ghost of an old tramp was supposed to haunt that road. So, did we see a ghost that night?
What gives you nightmares?
I always had a recurring dream about going home and my mother not letting me in because I was already there. I could see myself standing behind her.

ILLUSTRATOR FACT FILE
KAREN DONNELLY

Who is your favourite villain from a book or film?
Cruella DeVille, or any of the nasties in *Doctor Who* – I loved the drawings that came to life in the episode about the London Olympics! I also liked Gollum in the *Lord of the Rings*.

Do you believe in ghosts/aliens/monsters – any of the above?

I believe in ghostly 'feelings' and 'presences', and I don't see why there wouldn't be other life forms out there. I do feel spooked if I see a crop circle – why would anyone go to all that trouble for a joke?

What's the spookiest thing that has happened to you?
Once I had a very powerful dream about some friends I hadn't seen for a long time. The next day, they rang me up, which was a surprise anyway, and what I'd dreamed had actually just happened to them. It wasn't very nice either.

On a scale of one to ten, how scary are you?
One – not very! Unless you make me REALLY angry ...

Barrington Stoke would like to thank all its readers for commenting on the manuscript before publication and in particular:

Liliana Billing	Toinette Pardoe
Katie Douce	Jay Pettitt
Amy Gregg	Fergus Powell
Joshua French	Justin Smith
Ben Hancock	Jackie Tose
Pauline Liptrot	Lucy Whipp
April Lloyd	Rachel Wilks
Alwyn Martin	Nia Williams
Steven Murphy	Holly Woodnough
Kirstie Nisbet	

Become a Consultant!

Would you like to give us feedback on our titles before they are published? Contact us at the email address below – we'd love to hear from you!

info@barringtonstoke.co.uk
www.barringtonstoke.co.uk

Try another book in the "fyi" series! Fiction with stacks of facts

The Egyptians
The Three-Legged Mummy
by Vivian French

Rock Music
Diary of a Trainee Rock God
by Jonathan Meres

Boxing
The Greatest
by Alan Gibbons

All available from our website:
www.barringtonstoke.co.uk